Our Mommy
Works With Cars

Written by Melanie Borden

Illustrated by Annabelle King

Our Mommy
Works With Cars

Written by Melanie Borden

Illustrated by Annabelle King

Every day, our Mommy goes to a car dealership and she works with cars. A car dealership is a store that sells cars. Our Mommy works with a lot of other Mommies (and Daddies) too. Did you know, there are even Grandmas and Grandpas that work in car dealerships?

Our Mommy meets all kinds of nice people at the car dealership.

Our Mommy does a lot of her work on a computer. She uses her computer for social media to send messages to families, so they will come in to buy cars.

Some of the cars are really fast, and some are slow.

Mommy likes to visit with Naomi in the service department. Naomi helps with making appointments for people to bring in their cars to get fixed. Naomi is also a Mommy. Mommy and Naomi are friends who work together!

There are people our Mommy and Naomi work with in the service department who make your car shiny, and sparkly. They do car makeovers. They
clean your car, and make it smell really nice, like flowers.

Did you know that Adam's Mommy, Katie, fixes the cars? Katie makes sure the cars are safe to drive kids around in. Mommies can do so many cool things!

There is an office upstairs where they keep all of the paperwork for the cars. There are Mommies who work in the office. They have calculators to do math when they sell cars.

Sometimes, we get to go to Mommy's office. We get to sit at Mommy's desk and color in pictures of princesses and decorate the office. We feel so lucky.

Our Mommy takes us to meet the people she works with. They are so nice to Mommy and us. Everyone smiles. It feels so special that we feel like superstars!

Josie works in the showroom where people come to see the shiny new cars for sale. She helps families find new cars to buy. Josie is a Grandma, and always gives us big hugs.

Our Mommy lets us be silly, spinning around in the showroom. We spin around the beautiful sparkly cars.

Dina is a custodian. That means she makes the dealership floors sparkle. Dina is also an artist, so she knows how to make things shine.

We want to be like our Mommy and work at a car dealership when we grow up.

ABOUT THE AUTHOR

MELANIE BORDEN has spent the majority of her marketing career in the automotive tech industry. Melanie has worked in various atmospheres from social media startups to a public tech company in consulting, marketing, and business development roles. She has driven marketing efficiencies for her clients along the eastern seaboard from NYC to Burlington, VT. Melanie is the driver for the marketing vision and strategy from inception to execution for the clients she has worked with. Presently, she is the Vice President of Marketing for Celebrity Motor Cars, a franchised highline auto group based out of the New York and New Jersey Metropolitan area. Melanie develops and implements every single facet of the marketing and advertising strategy, and singlehandedly built the in-house advertising agency.

You can reach Melanie at www.melanieborden.com

CPSIA information can be obtained
at www.ICGtesting.com
Printed in the USA
LVHW011054100221
678898LV00007B/683

9 781087 883748